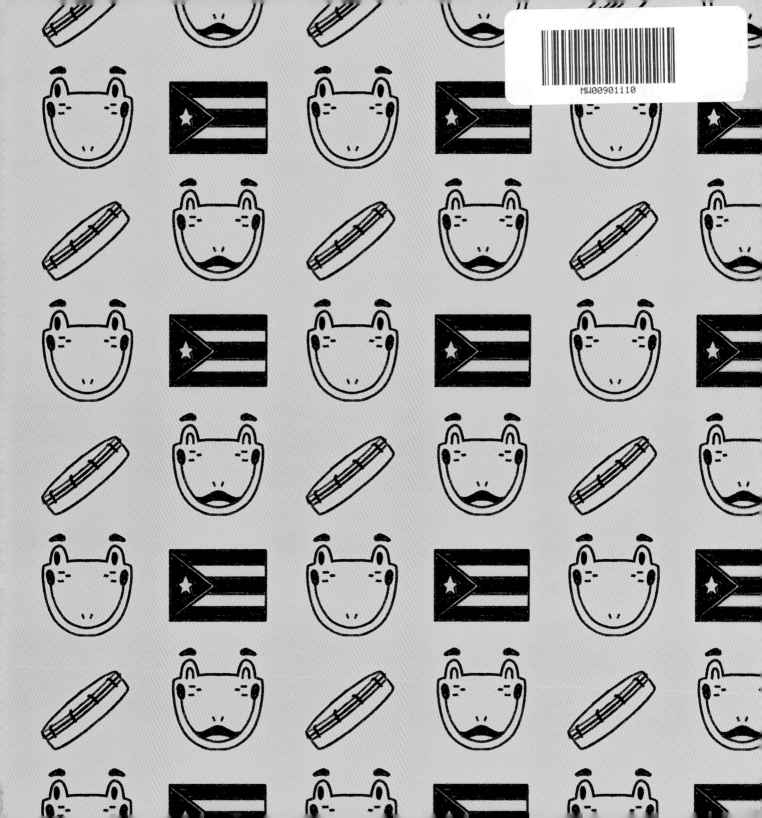

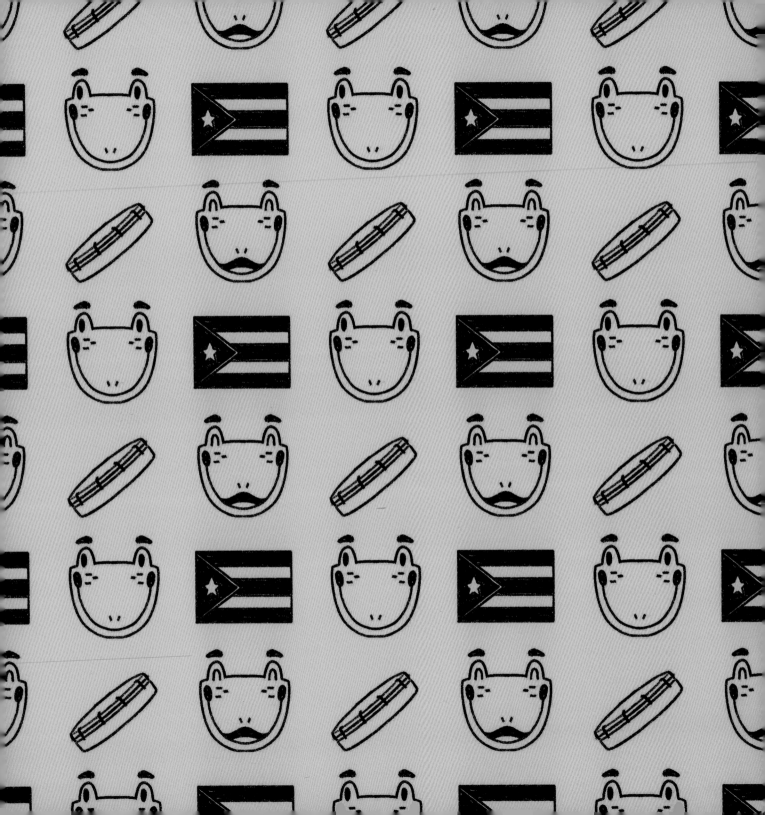

ROQUÍ'S PANDERO BEAT

To My friend TY! :")
Happy Reading -ö-
♡ Delia GyR

Delia Ruiz

Illustrated by Luis Patiño

To all the students I have taught, you have all touched and inspired me.

....

Para todos los estudiantes qué he tenido la oportunidad de educar.

Roqui's Pandero Beat

Copyright 2021
Written by Delia Ruiz
Illustrated by Luis Patiño

Library of Congress Control Number: 2020925937

978-1-7364093-0-5 (Paperback)

978-0-578-74275-5 (Hardcover)

Ba-dum-dum-dum echoed a beat through Roquí's door. Roquí hopped out of bed to the usual morning sound.

In the kitchen sat Papá Coquí's *pandero* drum as he was enjoying *café con pan* for breakfast.

"*Café con pan*," said Roquí as he started moving his fingers.

He ran the words through his mind tapping out the rhythm *ca-fé-con-pan, ca-fé-con-pan*.

Roquí dreamed of the day he would perform as a *pandero* drummer like *papá*. All he had to find now were friends to play with, but who would want to play music with a tiny frog?

"*Vámonos,*" said Mamá Coquí from around the corner. "It's time to go. Your *papá* got a new job. The plane is waiting for us to go to New York."

Roquí had never left the island before. "I wonder if New York has *panderos*," he thought.

Roquí packed the most important item, his favorite drum.

His tummy was full of butterflies as the plane approached.

He pulled his *papá's pandero* to calm his nerves. *Ca-fé-con-pan* played Roquí.

Roquí's *familia* boarded the plane to New York. He watched as the island got smaller and smaller until it was no more than a tiny dot below.

"*Adiós*, Puerto Rico," sighed Roquí.

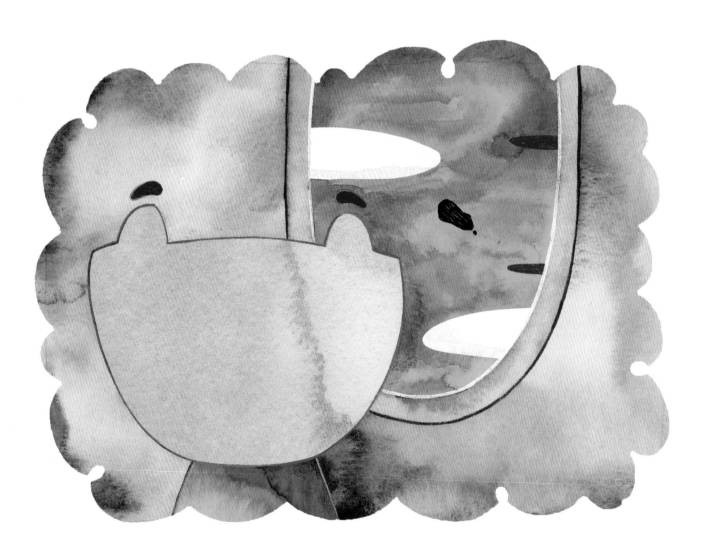

New York City was so different from Puerto Rico. *"Es grande,"* gasped Roquí.

"*Sí*," said Mamá Coquí, "and your new school is big too. You start tomorrow morning."

While Roquí waited for the school bus, he could feel his palms sweating. He tried to distract himself.

Ca-fé-con-pan, he tapped. *Ca-fé-con-pan*, he clapped.

When he entered the classroom he noticed he was the smallest student there.

He tried not to focus on being such a tiny frog. Instead, he drummed away on his desk. *Ca-fé-con-pan*, he tapped with his pencil.

READY
SET
READ!

"Is that a new song?" asked Koala.

"It's just a beat, but maybe one day it will become a big hit," replied Roquí.

"Nice! Come on, let's go to the rug for story time!" exclaimed Koala.

"Class, tell your partner something you want to be when you grow up," said Miss Pigeon.

"I want to be a dancer," twirled Koala.

"I want to be a boxer," said Rabbit, punching the air in front of her.

"We want to play *bomba* music," said the iguana triplets.

"I want to play *plena* music," Roquí announced.

"You can't," said the iguanas. "You're too small to play, plus we already play the best genre of music from Puerto Rico."

Roquí felt *frustrado*. He headed for the bathroom slowly hopping out of rhythm on the way: *ca-fé-con-pan*, he bounced. "*Café con pan*," Roquí whispered.

"*Hola, amigo,*" said Parrot. "*Estás bien?* What's wrong?"

"I want to be a *pandero* drummer but I'm just a tiny frog," answered Roquí. "I'm too small to play a big part."

"Nonsense," said Parrot, "being a musician doesn't have to do with size, it has to do with having passion. Do you have a *pandero* you can bring to play *plena*?"

The next day, Roquí brought his *papá's* drum to show and tell. "This is a *pandero.* It's a hand drum from my home in Puerto Rico," Roquí explained. "Repeat after me: *café-con-pan, café-con-pan.*"

The students sounded out each syllable together.

"It means 'coffee with bread.' That's a breakfast I enjoy back home— but it's also a phrase that helps me keep the beat while I drum!"

"Now tap with me. *Ca-fé-con-pan, ca-fé-con-pan*," Roquí drummed.

His classmates drummed and tapped to the beat. They joined a circle around Roquí and clapped together: *ca-fé-con-pan, ca-fé-con-pan.*

Even the iguanas were clapping and dancing to the beat.
"*Me gusta*," thought the first iguana.

"I think this beat will work great with *bomba* music," said the second iguana.

"Let's play music together!" blurted the third iguana.

"Roquí, will you join us to play?" the iguana triplets pleaded.

Roquí's eyes lit up.

As the class continued to clap and sing along, Miss Pigeon encouraged Roquí and the iguanas to play at the Puerto Rican parade, the *Parada Puertorriqueña.*

"You both can play *bomba* and *plena* together—two of Puerto Rico's great musical genres," she suggested.

On *sábado*, Roquí put on his favorite shirt, grabbed his *papá's* drum, and headed to the Puerto Rican parade with an immeasurable smile.

When he approached, he saw the iguana trio wave to invite him over to join. As the music played, Roquí drummed away focused on the beat. He swirled around, tapping out his rhythm: *ca-fé-con-pan*, *ca-fé-con-pan*.

Roquí and his new friends played *bomba* and *plena*, their rhythms joining in harmony.

As the day went on, they played in unity to the sound of the beat.

Glossary

adiós [ah-dee-ohs]—Goodbye

amigo [uh-mee-goh]—Friend

bomba [bohm-bah]—Afro-Puerto Rican musical genre

café-con-pan [kah-fe kohn pahn]—Coffee with bread

coquí [koe-kee]—Species of frog native to Puerto Rico

es grande [es grahn-deh]— It's big

estás bien [ehs-tahs bee-ehn]—Are you okay

familia [fah-mee-lyah]—Family

frustrado [froos-trah-doh]—Frustrated

hola [oh-lah]—Hello

mamá [mah-mah]—Mom

me gusta [meh goos-tah]—I like it

pandero [pahn-deh-roh]—Handheld drum from Puerto Rico

papá [pah-pah]—Dad

Parada Puertorriqueña [pah-rah-dah pwer-toh-rree-keh-nyah]—Puerto Rican parade

plena [pleh-nah]—Afro-Puerto Rican musical genre

Roquí [roe-kee]—Name of the main character in this book

sábado [sah-bah-doh]—Saturday

sí [see]—Yes

vámonos [bah-moh-nohs]—Let's go

About the Author

Delia Ruiz is an educator and writer. This is her first book of many more to come. Delia enjoys traveling, visiting local coffee shops, and dancing. She resides in San Diego, California with her husband and two pugs. You can follow her journey at:

 @aventuras.en.esl

aventurasenesl.com

#RoquisPanderoBeat

About the Illustrator

Luis Patiño is an artist based in Grapevine, Texas. Some of his favorite things include plants, hiking, and traveling. You can follow his journey at:

 @nino_planta

ninoplanta.com

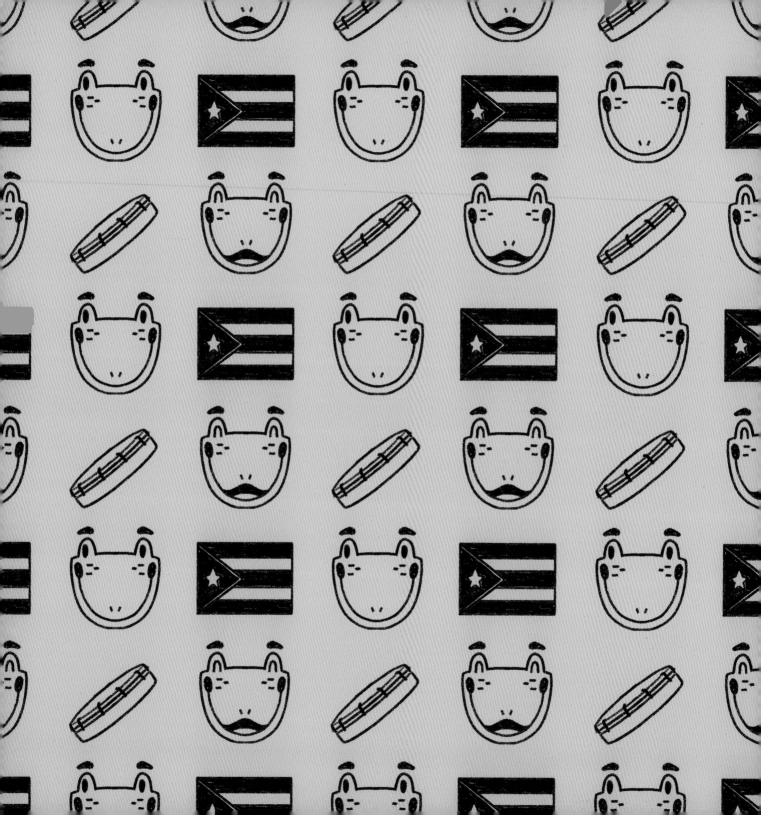